THE UNICORNS OF SPARKLE VALLEY
Moon Magic

Published in the UK by Scholastic, 2025
Scholastic, Bosworth Avenue, Warwick, CV34 6UQ

SCHOLASTIC and associated logos are trademarks and/or
registered trademarks of Scholastic Inc.

Text © Catherine Coe, 2025
Illustrations by Ryan Ball © Scholastic, 2025
Cover illustration by Ilias Arahovitis © Scholastic, 2025

The right of Catherine Coe to be identified as the author of this work has been asserted by them
under the Copyright, Designs and Patents Act 1988.

ISBN 978 0702 33866 3

A CIP catalogue record for this book is available from the British Library.

All rights reserved.
This book is sold subject to the condition that it shall not, by way of trade or otherwise, be lent,
hired out or otherwise circulated in any form of binding or cover other than that in which it is published.
No part of this publication may be reproduced, stored in a retrieval system, or transmitted in
any form or by any other means (electronic, mechanical, photocopying, recording or otherwise) or
used to train any artificial intelligence technologies) without prior written permission of
Scholastic Limited. Subject to EU law Scholastic Limited expressly reserves this work from the text
and data mining exception.

Printed in the UK
Paper made from wood grown in sustainable forests and other controlled sources.

1 3 5 7 9 10 8 6 4 2

This is a work of fiction. Any resemblance to actual people, events or locales is entirely coincidental.

www.scholastic.co.uk

For safety or quality concerns:
UK: www.scholastic.co.uk/productinformation
EU: www.scholastic.ie/productinformation

The Unicorns of Sparkle Valley

Moon Magic

Catherine Coe

For Emma xxx

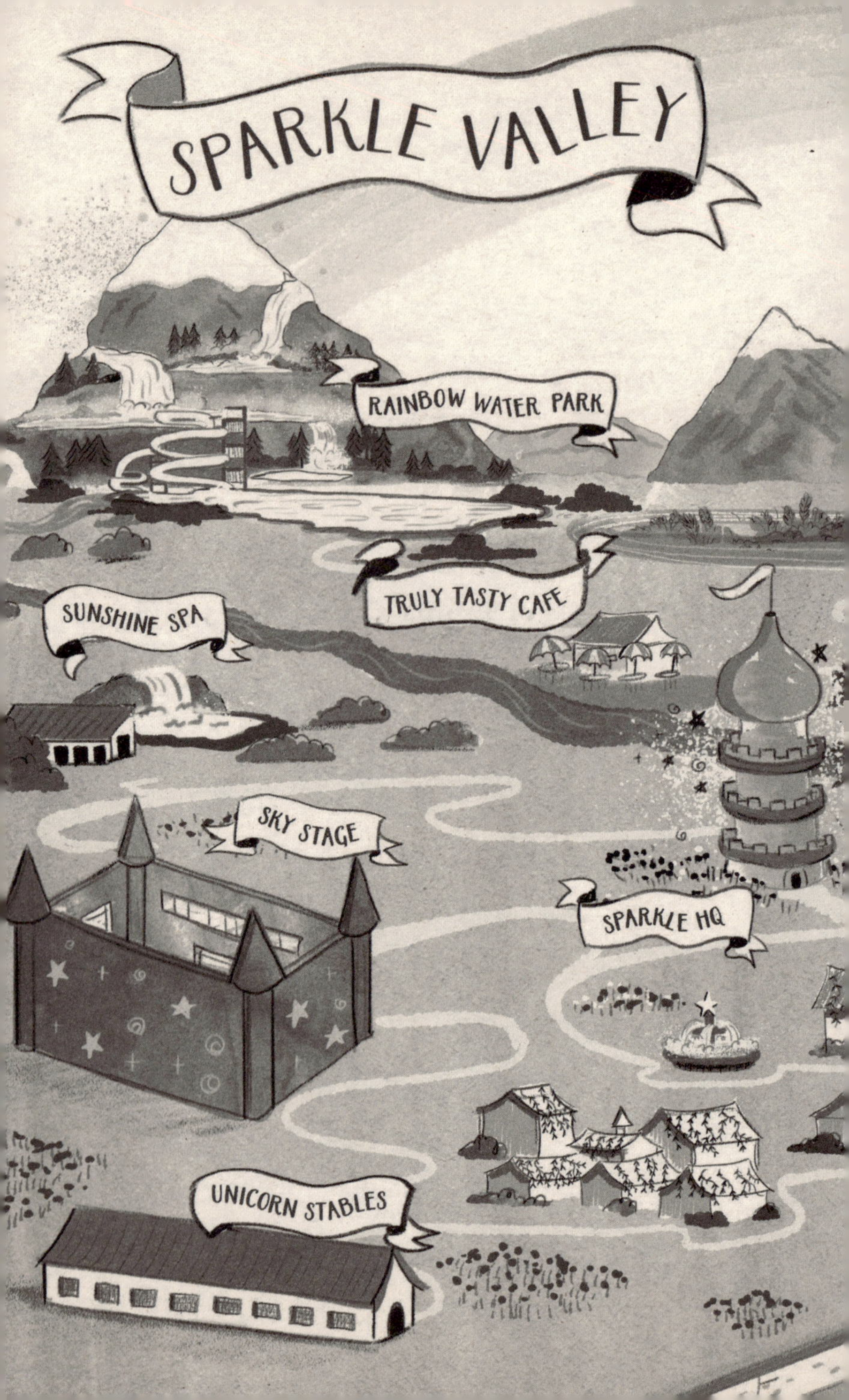
SPARKLE VALLEY
RAINBOW WATER PARK
TRULY TASTY CAFE
SUNSHINE SPA
SKY STAGE
SPARKLE HQ
UNICORN STABLES

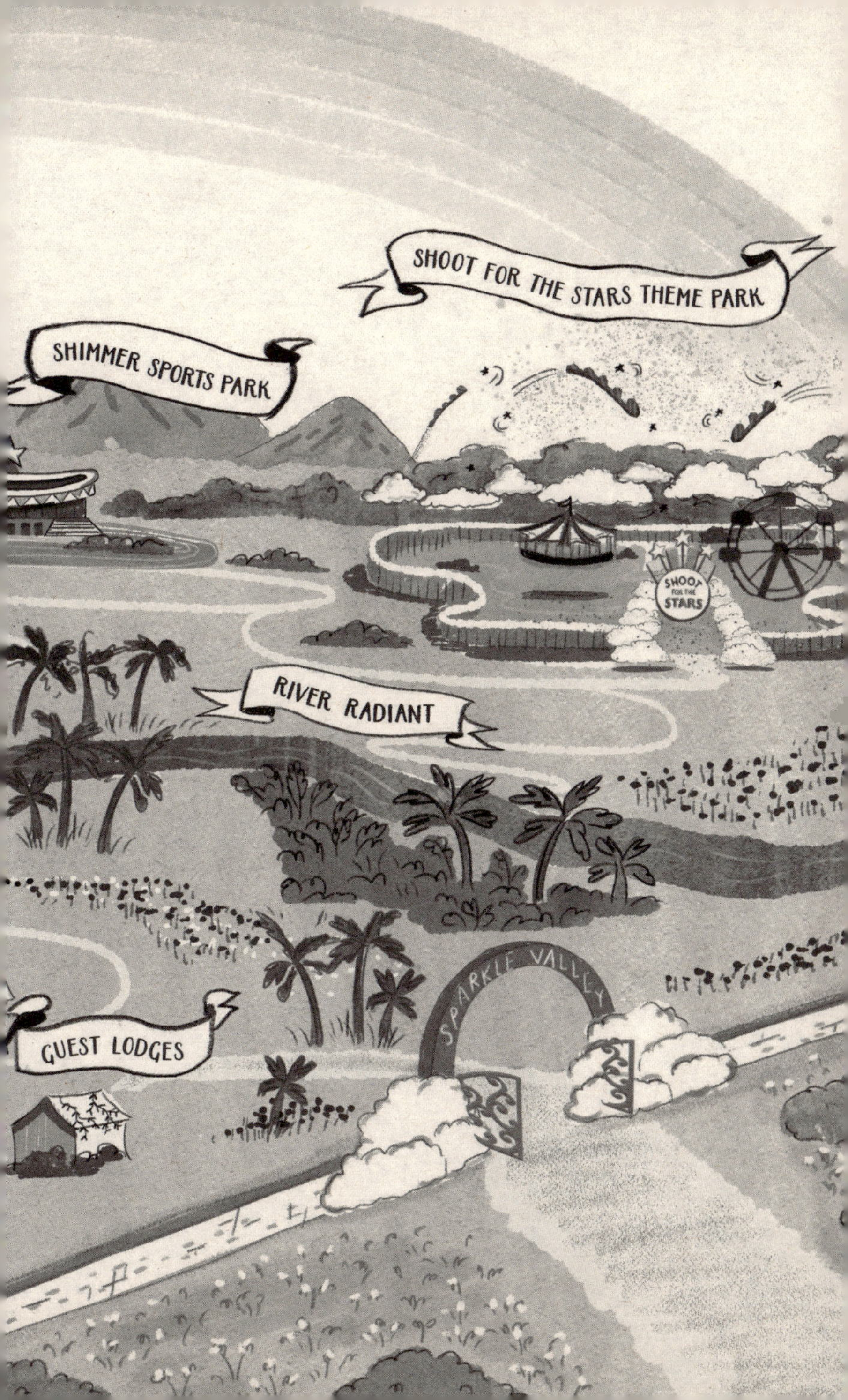
SHOOT FOR THE STARS THEME PARK
SHIMMER SPORTS PARK
SHOOT FOR THE STARS
RIVER RADIANT
SPARKLE VALLEY
GUEST LODGES

Chapter 1

Ming's Moon Jump

Ming the moon rabbit scooped up her moon-shaped backpack and hopped out of her lodge at Sparkle Valley. She'd had a wonderful time at the magical holiday park run by unicorns, but she was looking forward to getting home to her warren on the moon, where she lived by herself.

She scampered out of her lodge, smiling as she spotted the River Radiant glistening in the distance. At the beginning of her holiday, she'd learned to kayak on the river with Indigo, one of the unicorns. Ming had enjoyed it so much that she'd kayaked every day since, getting up early to enjoy the river before it got busy with

the other guests. There were no rivers on the moon, but that still didn't make Ming want to stay on Earth. She was used to living alone and, despite how much fun she'd had at Sparkle Valley, she couldn't help but feel homesick for her quiet, calm life among the stars.

As Ming hopped along the main avenue, which was lined with sparkling palm trees, she spotted all the unicorns at the end of the path, by the entrance to Sparkle Valley. They were bidding goodbye to a few other magical creatures who were leaving too. Ming could see a couple of young trolls with tears in their eyes, clearly upset to leave. Ming felt bad for them, especially when her own silver tummy fluttered with excitement at the thought of going home.

"Ming," said Scarlett, the unicorn

in charge of magic at Sparkle Valley. "Thank you for visiting Sparkle Valley!" She beamed and put out a hoof to shake Ming's paw, as her red tail swooshed from side to side.

Ming smiled as she shook Scarlett's hoof. "Thank you for having me," she said. "Sparkle Valley really is the most magical place in the universe."

The unicorns all grinned at that, because that was their resort's slogan. And while it *was* the most magical place Ming had been to, there was nothing like going back to the comfort and familiarity of home.

She looked up at the moon: a faint white slice in the bright blue sky. Ming could already imagine how it would feel to be back on the cool lunar surface, surrounded by bright stars and watching the blue and green circle of Earth as the moon moved slowly round it.

Ming hopped through the shimmering silver gates, waving back at the unicorns. Just outside the entrance, she planted her feet firmly on the ground, getting ready to leap up and shoot towards the moon. She waggled her long ears, sending sparks of magic out from the tips. Crouching down to take off, Ming then leaped into the air, high above the unicorns and ...

... landed back on the ground again.

Ming looked down at her rear feet and frowned. Concentrating hard, she crouched again, this time even lower, and waggled her ears faster than ever before. The air filled with silver moon-rabbit magic, bursting from her ear-tips like a sparkler. Ming looked up at the moon in the distance, pushed down into her heels and jumped, reaching her front paws forward this time to help her fly upwards. But, again, she landed on the ground.

When Ming had jumped down to Earth to get to Sparkle Valley, it'd been easy. She'd leaped off the moon's surface and flown through space, her moon magic easily propelling her downwards. So what was wrong now?

"Is everything OK?" Scarlett asked, trotting towards her.

Ming looked up. "My moon magic…" she said, shaking her head. "It's not working!"

Scarlett looked from Ming to the moon and back again. She'd seen Ming when she'd landed outside the gates to Sparkle Valley a week ago. Her jump from the moon had looked effortless.

The unicorn raised her front hooves

and began rubbing them together, until sparks of magic fizzed from her horn.

"Let me help," Scarlett offered. "Maybe you just need a little more magic today."

She sent the magical sparks towards Ming as the moon rabbit crouched again and wriggled her ears.

Scarlett held her breath as Ming leaped up … and came crashing down once more, falling on to her fluffy silver tail.

Ming put her paws to her eyes. "I don't know what's wrong," she said, beginning to sob. "I just want to get back to the moon. It was so easy when I came here last week!"

Indigo – the unicorn in charge of safety – cantered over. "Was there anything different when you jumped down to Earth last week?" they asked.

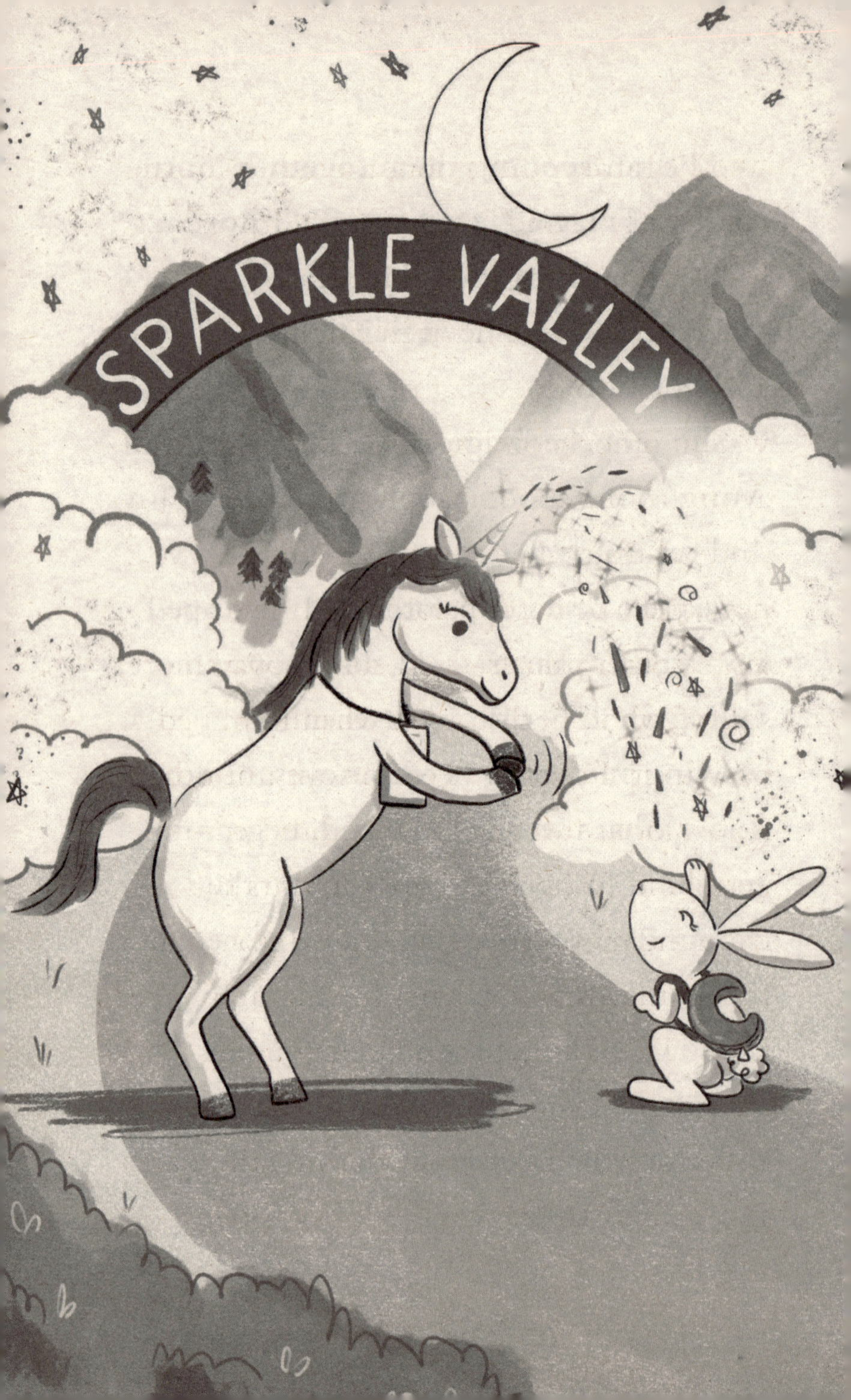
SPARKLE VALLEY

"Well, from the moon, the Earth looked completely round," Ming said. "It was beautiful – so bright and blue…"

Indigo screwed up their forehead in thought. "So does that mean you'll have to wait another month for the Earth to be full again from the moon?"

Ming considered that for a moment. "I've never been to Earth before, but I have visited other planets, and I could always see the whole of the moon when I jumped back to it. I think I need to wait until the moon looks full from *here* before I can get home. When the Earth appears full from the moon, *you* have a new moon on Earth, meaning you can't see the moon at all. Then, as the moon gets rounder and brighter for you on Earth, I see the opposite from the moon. For me, the Earth gradually disappears – while you slowly start to see more of the moon…"

Scarlett nodded. "Ah, in that case, it would have been a new moon here last week and it takes two weeks from then to become a full moon. That means you'll have to wait another week to get back. Is that right?"

"Uh-huh," replied Ming, lowering her head to her fluffy silver chest.

She couldn't say any more because her throat was tight with sadness. As much as she'd enjoyed Sparkle Valley, she'd been looking forward to returning to her cosy home, and now she'd have to wait a whole extra week! She tipped her head up to gaze longingly at the half-moon above.

"I'm sorry, Ming," Indigo said. "Please come and stay with us for another week. There's plenty of space, because the atotolin birds had to delay their visit to Sparkle

Valley as they all have bird flu. We'll make sure you have another fun-filled week here, I promise!"

Ming slowly got to her paws and tried to smile. She knew she shouldn't complain. Most creatures would do anything to spend an extra week at Sparkle Valley. But Ming liked her own company and was ready to be by herself again.

As she hopped alongside the unicorns, back through the entrance to the park, all Ming could think about was getting back home. She only hoped she was right about the full moon and that she just had to wait another week. But what if she couldn't get back to the moon at all?

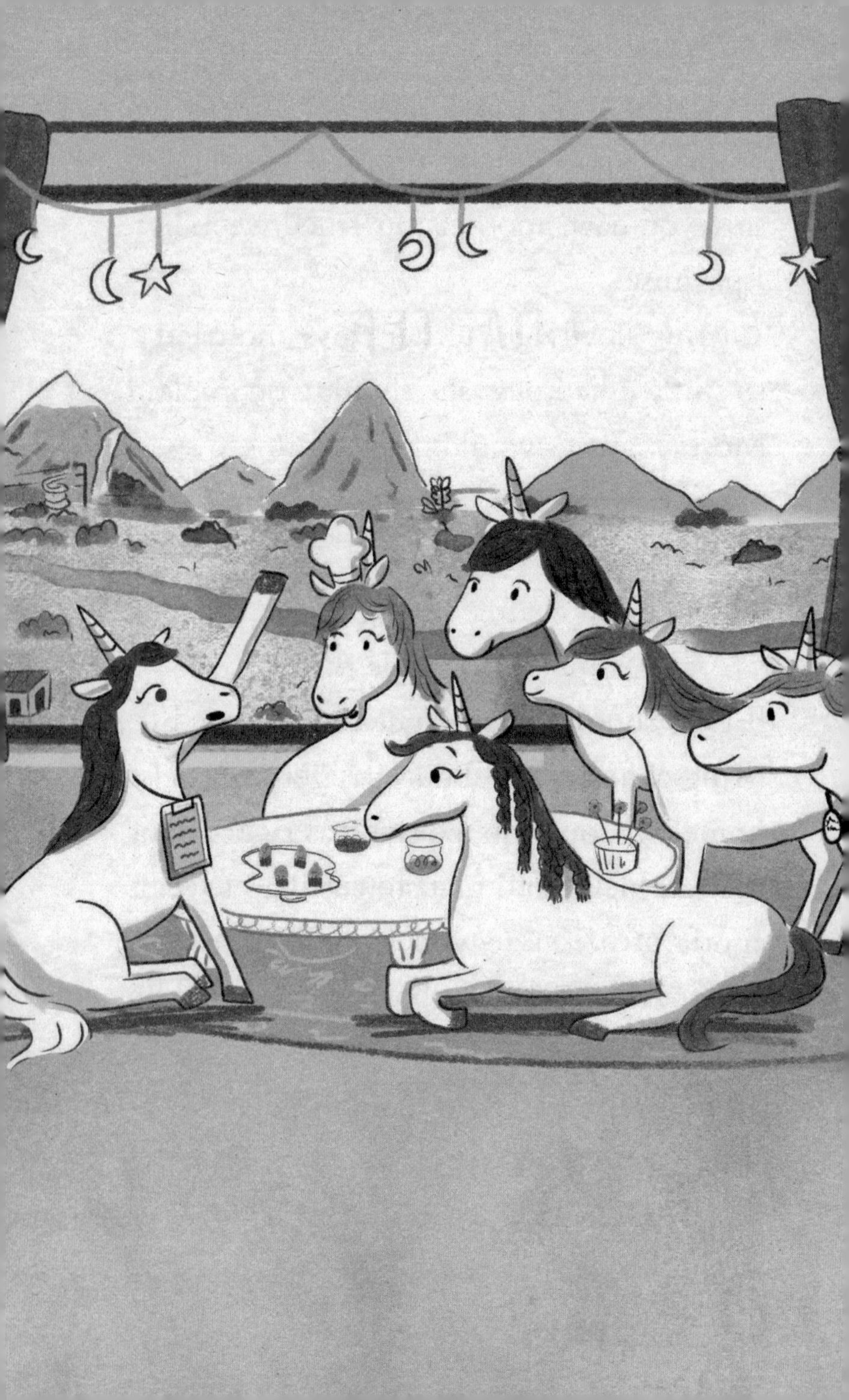

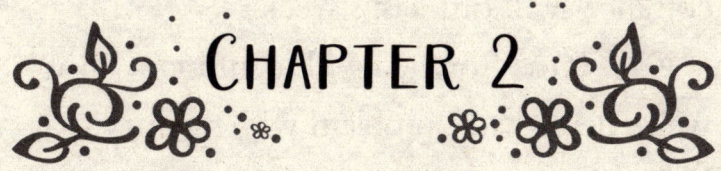

Chapter 2

A Great Idea

The next morning, the unicorns gathered together for their usual weekly meeting at Sparkle HQ – a silver tower in the middle of Sparkle Valley. From the top room, which had floor-to-ceiling windows, they could see across the whole of the holiday park, sparkling with magic in the sunshine.

Scarlett raised a hoof to start. "All the guests arrived safely yesterday, apart from the atotolins, who have been delayed."

Indigo nodded. "And the griffins have requested that two of them stand guard at the entrance at all times this week."

Chef Rose frowned with confusion. "But we've never had a problem with security before, have we? Apart from the time Basil turned into a unicorn thief and pinched all the candyfloss strawberries I'd made for the May Day party…"

Basil lowered his head. "I'm sorry – they were so tasty, though. I didn't realize they were for the party!"

Rose winked. "I'm kidding, Basil. I was flattered you liked them so much, and you helped me make more anyway. I'm only teasing. I couldn't resist mentioning it – Basil the burglar!"

Basil gave a guilty smile and all the unicorns laughed.

Scarlett looked at Indigo. "So are the

griffins worried about anything in particular?"

Indigo smiled. "I don't think so. They're just used to protecting everyone and everything. It's what griffins are known for. I got the impression it would make them happy to act as our security guards this week!"

"Well, if it makes them happy, why not?" Scarlett said, smiling back.

"I've been preparing tons of cactus juice specially for the pair of cactus cats that we have with us," Rose said, pulling a face. "Personally, it tastes like month-old bog water to me, and it smells as bad, but they requested it!"

Lightning nodded. He was in charge of Creature Comforts, always making sure every visitor to Sparkle Valley had everything they needed to enjoy their holiday here. "It's the only thing they'll drink," he said. "So please make sure you have enough, Rose!"

Rose raised a hoof to her forehead in a mock salute. Lightning could be pretty bossy at times, but she knew it was only because he took his job very seriously. Meanwhile, Rose liked to laugh and joke as much as possible. She figured that life was so much better if you focused on the fun things!

"We do have an extra here this week, as you all know," Scarlett continued. "Ming the moon rabbit wasn't able to get back home." She turned to the window and spotted Ming, who was kayaking along the River Radiant. "Oh, look – there she is!"

Indigo lifted a hoof to speak. "I'm a little worried about Ming," they said. "It was obvious she was looking forward to going back home. She's used to living on her own, you see. I know everyone likes a holiday, but it can also be really lovely to return home afterwards. I think

Ming's a bit upset about it all."

Deep down, Indigo was worried about the promise they'd made to Ming about making sure she had another fun-filled week here. What if they couldn't cheer her up?

"Then we should do something to help!" said Basil, jumping up and clicking his rear hooves together. He was the Entertainment Officer after all. "If we keep her busy, she won't feel so homesick."

"That's a good idea," said Scarlett. "Does anyone have any suggestions?"

The unicorns all went quiet for a moment as they thought hard about what they could do for Ming.

Amber broke the silence. "I could do some special spa treatments for her," she suggested. Amber ran the Sunshine Spa in Sparkle Valley, and loved nothing more than giving creatures sumptuous spa treatments to make them feel relaxed and peaceful.

"How lovely," said Scarlett with a flick of her tail. "I might have to join her – my back's been aching recently. I'd love one of your deep-tissue massages."

"Sure thing!" said Amber, spinning on the spot.

Lightning put a hoof to his chin. "Your spa treatments are excellent, Amber, but will they keep Ming busy all week? She might not want to be in the spa all the time…"

"I know," Basil said, suddenly jumping from hoof to hoof. "We could hold a sports day!"

Lightning clapped his hooves. "Oh, yes – that's a great idea!"

"We could put everyone in teams," Basil went on. "They can spend the next few days preparing, and we'll hold the sports day just before they leave at the end of the week. It'll be so much fun!" He looked around at his fellow unicorns. "Don't you think?"

Lightning was beaming, and the other unicorns began nodding too.

"It does sound like a good way to keep Ming busy and having fun," said Scarlett.

"And I can still give her lots of spa treatments!" added Amber, tapping her front hooves together.

"I can make lots of yummy sports-day food," suggested Rose. "Everyone will need lots of energy if they're competing!"

"We'll have to be careful, of course," Indigo said. "I want to make sure all the sports are safe – and accessible and inclusive too. We have a star-nosed mole staying with us this week, so he may need a guide to compete in some of the sports, as he's blind."

"Good thinking," Scarlett replied. She

picked up her clipboard from the table and began writing with her firebird-feather pen. "As well as Ming, this will keep us very busy too. We've never had a sports day before!"

"It'll be brilliant," said Basil. "Let's make it the best sports day ever!"

Chapter 3

A Sporty Announcement

Ming was eating a delicious dessert of meteor-munch mousse at Truly Tasty, the outdoor revolving restaurant by the river, when an announcement came over the loudspeakers.

"Hello, all creatures, this is Scarlett. I hope you're having a wonderful time at Sparkle Valley so far. The other unicorns and I would like to invite you all to a special meeting at two o'clock at Shimmer

Sports Park. It's important that you come if you can. See you there!"

Everyone in the restaurant began talking. At the next table, Ming overheard a bunyip talking about whether something serious had happened.

"Maybe they always have a meeting like this," another bunyip suggested. They were large hippo-like creatures, with flippers and dog-like faces. "It's our first full day here, after all."

"But it wasn't mentioned in our welcome pack," the first bunyip said. "Maybe something's gone wrong. Maybe we'll have to leave. But we've only just arrived!"

Has something bad happened? Ming thought. She'd already been worrying whether she'd be able to get home at the end of this week, but now this new worry took over. She looked at the cuckoo-cutie clock in the restaurant. It was ten minutes to two o'clock, so at least she didn't have to wait very long to find out.

She ate the last mouthful of her mousse, swallowing it slowly to enjoy it, then wiped her mouth with the sparkling star-shape napkin. She loved how the napkins here magically removed all dirt and stickiness, and considered asking Chef Rose if she could take some home. Everyone in the restaurant was making their way out, but Ming waited, wanting to avoid the crowds.

When only Ming was left, she stood up and followed the train of creatures heading towards the Shimmer Sports Park. The arena at the sports park's centre was huge and circular – to Ming, it looked almost as big as the moon – and then she remembered that Scarlett magically changed its size and shape depending on what sport was being played inside. She'd watched a Twirl Tennis match between two elves last week, and it had been much smaller and rectangular then!

Ming found a free seat towards the back of the packed arena. The seats changed shaped too, of course, so they'd fit each size of creature, even the Loch Ness Monster, who was sitting over the other side, their long neck stretching up towards the roof.

The unicorns that ran the park were already on the circular stage in the middle. It seemed to shimmer with rainbow-coloured magic, as if they were standing on a magic platform that might whisk them up at any moment.

The unicorn with a green mane and tail held the microphone to his mouth. "Thank you all for coming to this meeting. In case you don't know me, I'm Basil, the

Entertainment Officer here in Sparkle Valley. I have some very important news for you." He paused for dramatic effect, and everyone seemed to hold their breath.

"This will be a very special week," Basil continued, "which we hope will provide more entertainment than ever before... We are going to hold the first-ever Sparkle Valley Sports Day!"

The entire arena seemed to sigh with relief, as all the creatures realized there was nothing to worry about. Many began chattering excitedly, until Lightning took the microphone and coughed into it to get the crowd's attention again.

"Ahem! As Basil said, we want to make this a very special week," Lightning said. "The sports day will be held at the end of this week and we're going to put you into teams, so that no one is left out – especially the creatures

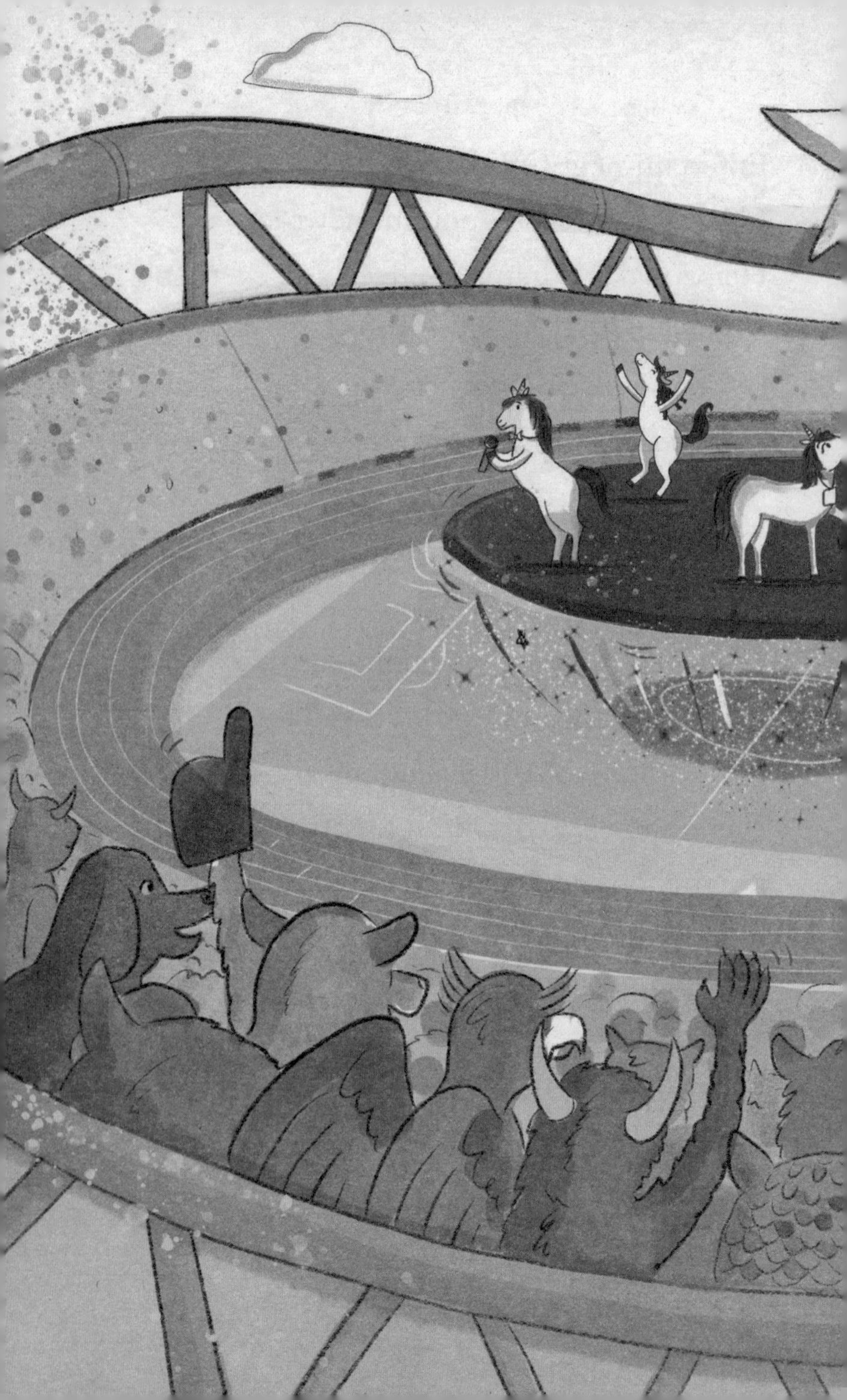

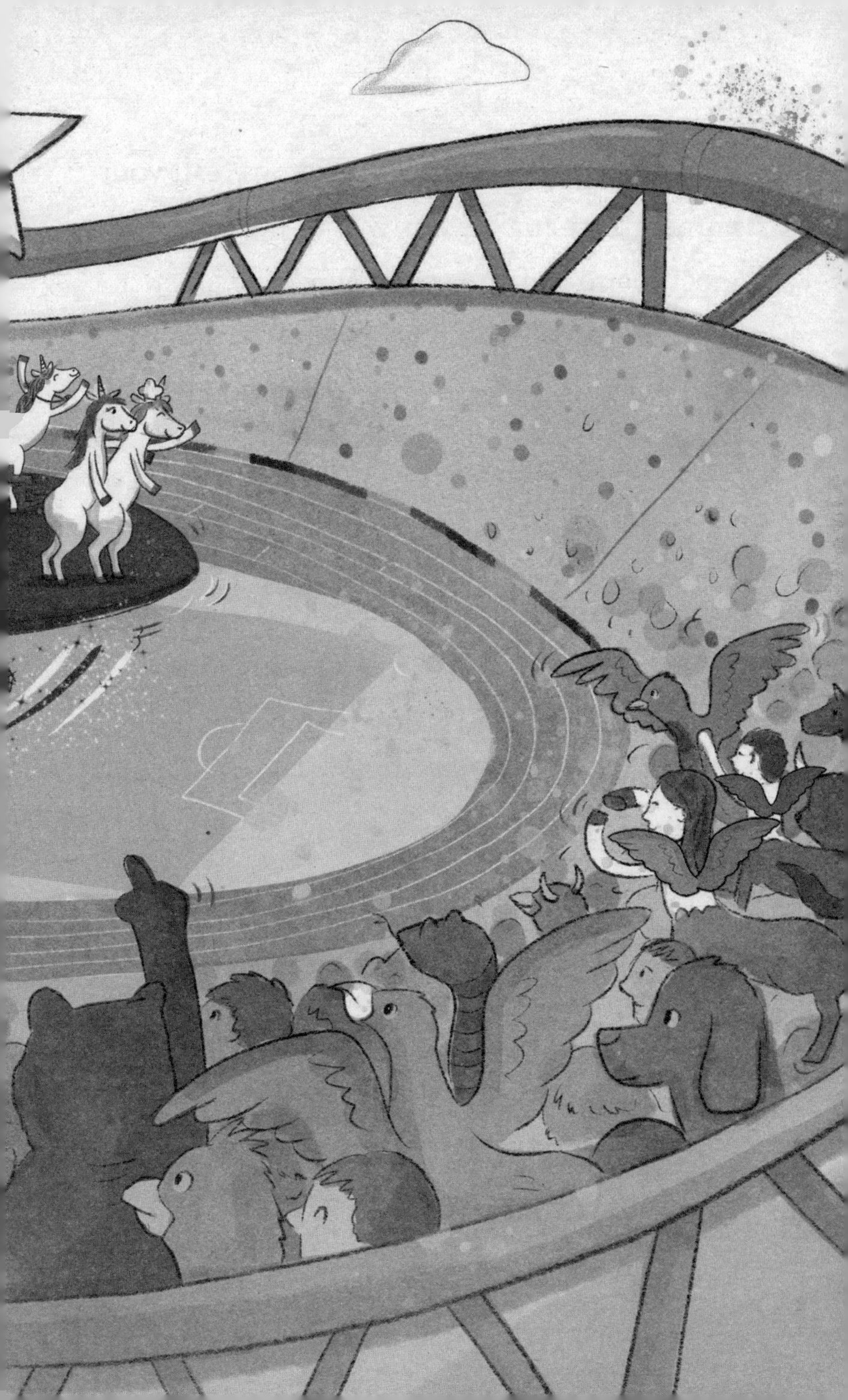

who are visiting us alone. When we call your name, please make your way to the stage to meet the rest of your team. We'll give you a list of the sports you'll be playing, so you can start practising together in preparation for the big day."

Ming suddenly felt very small. The thought of a sports day sounded fun, but she didn't know any of the other guests. Plus, she'd never played a sport before. After all, she didn't have anyone to play sports with back on the moon. She didn't *think* she was a very sporty person. But she had enjoyed the kayaking, and that was a sort of sport, she thought. So maybe she *was* sporty and just hadn't realized it. What did *sporty* mean, anyway? Would the other creatures mind that she hadn't played in a sports team before? Ming tried not to think about it too much and listened out for her name to be called.

One by one, names were announced. Eager guests gathered in small teams, then left the arena, chattering in excitement.

Eventually she heard her name. "Ming the moon rabbit!" Lightning called.

Fortunately the arena was much emptier now, with only a few creatures left, so it didn't feel too embarrassing to walk down to the shimmering multicoloured stage. Lightning beckoned Ming towards him and handed her the list of sports.

"You'll be in a team with the centaur family. Centaurs, come and join the lovely Ming!"

Ming looked up as the centaurs galloped towards the stage. With their silver horse legs and tails, impressive wings, and human bodies and heads, they looked big and strong. But they were smiling widely and waving to Ming, so she hoped they were friendly.

"Isn't this fantastic?" said one of the centaurs, trotting alongside Ming as they walked to the exit of the arena. "I'm Cecil!" He turned and pointed at the three centaurs behind him. "This is Serendipity, that's Cedric and that's Sirnam."

They all waved a hand and a hoof in greeting at Ming.

"Can I see the list, please?" Cedric asked, and Ming passed it to him. "Oh, look – we'll be doing a River Radiant swim – and there's

a Rainbow Relay too. This is going to be amazing. We're so going to win!"

"What sports do you play?" Serendipity asked Ming.

"I … erm… Well, I like kayaking," Ming said quietly.

"Kayaking?" Sirnam said. "Is that a sport?"

"It's not on the list," Cedric said, looking over it again. "What else?"

Ming looked at her paws. "I don't really play sports. I live by myself, you see. On the moon. I was supposed to be home by now, but I can't get back yet…"

But the centaurs had stopped listening. They were outside the arena now and crowding round the sports day list, chatting about which to practise first.

Ming's insides fluttered with nervousness but she tried not to show it. *It'll be OK*, she told herself. She'd try her best – and maybe she'd find out that she was really good at sports. It sounded like the centaurs were, and hopefully they'd be able to teach her…

Chapter 4

Hula High Jump

"Which sport would you like to practise first?" Cecil asked Ming. She wondered if the centaur had noticed she hadn't said anything for a while.

Ming checked the list. She hadn't heard of most of the sports, but one caught her eye: Hula High Jump. She was good at jumping – she just hadn't thought of it as a sport before!

"Oh yes, good choice," replied Serendipity

as Ming pointed to "Hula High Jump" on the list. The centaurs began galloping towards the edge of the sports park, where the athletics area was. It was a large empty space of rubber flooring.

Ming was confused. Where was the high jump?

She realized that the centaurs must have come to the sports park before, because Serendipity went to a shimmering pillar, waved a hand in the air and said, "Hula!" A second later, a high jump appeared in the corner, along with a stack of sparkling hula hoops.

Sirnam looked at the list of sports. "It says here that we have to jump over the high jump while spinning a hula hoop."

Before Sirnam could say anything else, Cedric had slipped a hula hoop over his waist and was trotting on the spot in front of the high-jump bar.

"It's magic!" Cedric said as he prepared for his jump. "The hula hoop is spinning without me doing anything!"

Ming was relieved to hear that. She could jump all right, but she'd never tried hula-hooping, and definitely not both together!

Cedric took a run towards the high jump and leaped far above the bar, his hooves reaching high into the sky as his wings flapped effortlessly. He landed on the other side, and Ming and the other centaurs clapped.

"Not bad," Cedric said. "But I'm sure I can do better next time. Ming, would you like to have a go next?"

Ming hopped forward, suddenly very nervous. She knew she could jump, but she didn't usually do it under pressure like this.

Ming tried not to think about the centaurs watching as she took a hula hoop and stepped into it. The hoop began spinning of its own accord, and Ming could feel bubbles of magic as it circled round her waist.

She walked close to the high jump and crouched, readying her legs and trying to put her last attempt at leaping to the moon out of her mind. *Now is not the time to think about going home*, she told herself. She waggled her ears, felt magic sparking out of the tips and used all her strength to leap towards the bar, watching as it passed just below her feet.

As Ming landed, the centaurs clapped politely, but she could tell that they didn't look particularly impressed.

"Don't worry," said Cecil. "It wasn't as high as Cedric, but you've got plenty of time to practise. We need to make sure we win, after all!"

Ming tried to smile, but she felt sad inside. She'd really tried her best with that jump.

The team spent the next hour practising the Hula High Jump and Ming quickly realized she'd never get as high as the centaurs when they had wings. It wasn't like on the moon, where there was less gravity – it was much easier to jump high there.

Ming was relieved when Serendipity

suggested they move on to a different sport.

"Good idea," said Sirnam. She looked at the list. "I've never tried Fizz-Foot Hockey, but it sounds fun, don't you think, Ming?"

Ming gazed up at the tall centaur. She hadn't heard of the sport, but she figured her big bunny feet would be an advantage. Really, Ming would much prefer going back to her lodge and relaxing, or taking a peaceful kayak ride along the River Radiant by herself, but she didn't want to let her team down.

The list of sports said that Fizz-Foot Hockey would be held in the arena, so they headed back there to practise. Basil was standing by the entrance, talking to creatures going in and out. He waved when he saw Ming and the centaurs.

"Are you having fun?" Basil asked, swishing his shimmering green tail.

"Oh yes," said Serendipity. "We've just been trying the Hula High Jump, and we're about to practise Fizz-Foot Hockey. We've never played it before, though…"

Basil beamed. "I'm sure you'll all pick it up quickly. It's a fast but simple sport! Ming, I hope it's keeping you busy. With all the sports day preparations, the time will go fast until you can get back home!"

Ming nodded as a thought pinged into her head. Had the unicorns organized the sports day to keep her distracted until she could get back to the moon? Indigo *had* promised to give her a fun-filled week, after all. It wasn't their fault that they didn't know this wasn't Ming's idea of fun…

"The arena is already set out for Fizz-Foot Hockey – or FFH, as we like to call it," Basil went on. "The team of gnomes and pixies are already inside. You could have a practice match with them. Enjoy!"

The centaurs trotted inside, Ming following behind. The arena was smaller now, with an oval grass pitch. At each end stood hockey nets, and in the centre circle was a large disc that fizzed with magic sparks. Ming guessed that was where the name Fizz-Foot Hockey came from.

The centaurs raced on to the pitch, waving to the pixies and gnomes. Ming was alarmed when she realized how fast they could run. She'd never keep up!

"Who's going in goal?" Sirnam asked. The centaurs looked at each other, no one volunteering.

This is my chance, Ming thought. *They won't see how bad I am at running if I'm in goal.*

"I'll do it," Ming said, and hopped towards one of the nets. It wasn't much bigger than her, so she hoped she'd be able to keep the fizzing disc out.

The practice game began, and at first Ming was very glad she'd offered to be in goal. The creatures kicked the disc so fast that it was a blur. She'd have never got a kick in! It seemed to switch directions as it spun in the air too, as if it had a mind of its own and was trying to catch the players off-guard. But then a pixie began running towards her with the disc, and panic rose in Ming's belly. Suddenly it was whizzing straight for her face, so fast she didn't have a chance to raise her paws in time to stop it…

"Ouch!" she yelled as it smacked her on the nose. Ming collapsed to the ground, holding her face.

"Are you OK?" asked Cecil as all the players ran over. "Don't worry – I can't see any blood."

"I'm so sorry!" said the pixie, who looked horrified that she'd hurt someone.

"Shall we stop the game?" Serendipity asked, crouching down to Ming.

The moon rabbit winced. She was glad she wasn't bleeding, but it still hurt, and she felt a bit dizzy. "No, you don't need to do that. But I think … maybe I should sit out for a while."

"But who will go in goal?" Cedric asked.

Sirnam prodded him. "Ming needs to rest, Cedric. One of us can go in goal for now."

Ming was relieved, but she felt bad too, for letting her team down already. How would she ever compete in the sports day if she was like this when they were only practising?

Chapter 5

Bouncing Around

The next morning, before any of their guests were awake, the unicorns met in the sports park arena.

"It's *so* early," said Indigo, rubbing their eyes and yawning.

Lightning swished his tail. "Yes, but we need to make sure this sports day is the best it can be! And anyway, I'm up this early *every* morning. The early firebird catches the worm and all that!"

Indigo looked at Lightning, confused. Why would anyone want to eat a worm? Weren't unicorns vegetarians?

"I know it's early," said Scarlett, "but we have to use the arena before any of the teams arrive. There's no other time when we'll be able to practise our synchronized sparkle trampolining."

It was the unicorns' own very special sport, but they didn't have much chance to practise when they were so busy running Sparkle Valley. They'd decided that they would make a show of it to begin the sports day, like an opening ceremony. So they had to fit in time to prepare, which meant getting up before the sun had even risen.

Scarlett had used magic to change the arena so it was filled with trampolines, enough for each of the unicorns. Chef Rose unclipped the cart attached to her back and lifted out some large glittery jugs and matching cups. "I brought along some super-sparkle-strawberry smoothies for us," she said, then winked. "There might be a bit of magic in them to give us all a boost of energy!"

"I definitely need one of those!" said Indigo.

Rose poured them a smoothie and Indigo gulped it down in one.

"Yummmmm!" they said. "I think I can feel it working already!" They shook their hooves and trotted towards one of the trampolines.

Each of the unicorns drank one of Rose's delicious smoothies before mounting a trampoline and beginning to jump.

Lightning led a warm-up, the unicorns copying him as he bounced on front legs, then back legs, then one leg at a time.

"Now we're really ready to get started!" he panted as the warm-up finished. "Can I show you all my suggestion for our performance?"

The other unicorns were very happy to take a rest while Lightning demonstrated. He turned to Scarlett. "Can we have some music, please?"

With a smile, Scarlett tapped her front hooves together, and gentle music magically began playing in the arena. She did a double-tap and the music changed to a faster song with trumpets and drums.

"Perfect!" said Lightning. He clapped his front hooves and started the piece, jumping and somersaulting and spinning, his legs flying up and down and side to side. As he moved, sparks shot out from his horn, whizzing around him to make the whole routine look even more magical.

Rose watched in both awe and horror. She'd never been the greatest at synchronized sparkle trampolining – she preferred spinning plates to spinning herself! Rose wondered if she'd ever be able to copy this, but she'd try her best!

Lightning's performance came to an end

with a final leap, quadruple spin and star jump. The unicorns clapped their hooves loudly and Lightning gave a low bow.

"That was wonderful," Scarlett said. "But we may have to make it a little more … gentle, if the rest of us are going to keep up and make it truly synchronized. We're not all as good at sparkle trampolining as you, Lightning!"

Rose breathed out in relief. Thank goodness Scarlett had said something.

Lightning began teaching them the routine, breaking down each section so it was easy to follow and clearly describing each move. Lightning might have been a bit bossy, but he was a really good teacher, Rose realized. She quickly picked up the first part of the routine, and surprised herself as she remembered how much she enjoyed it. There was

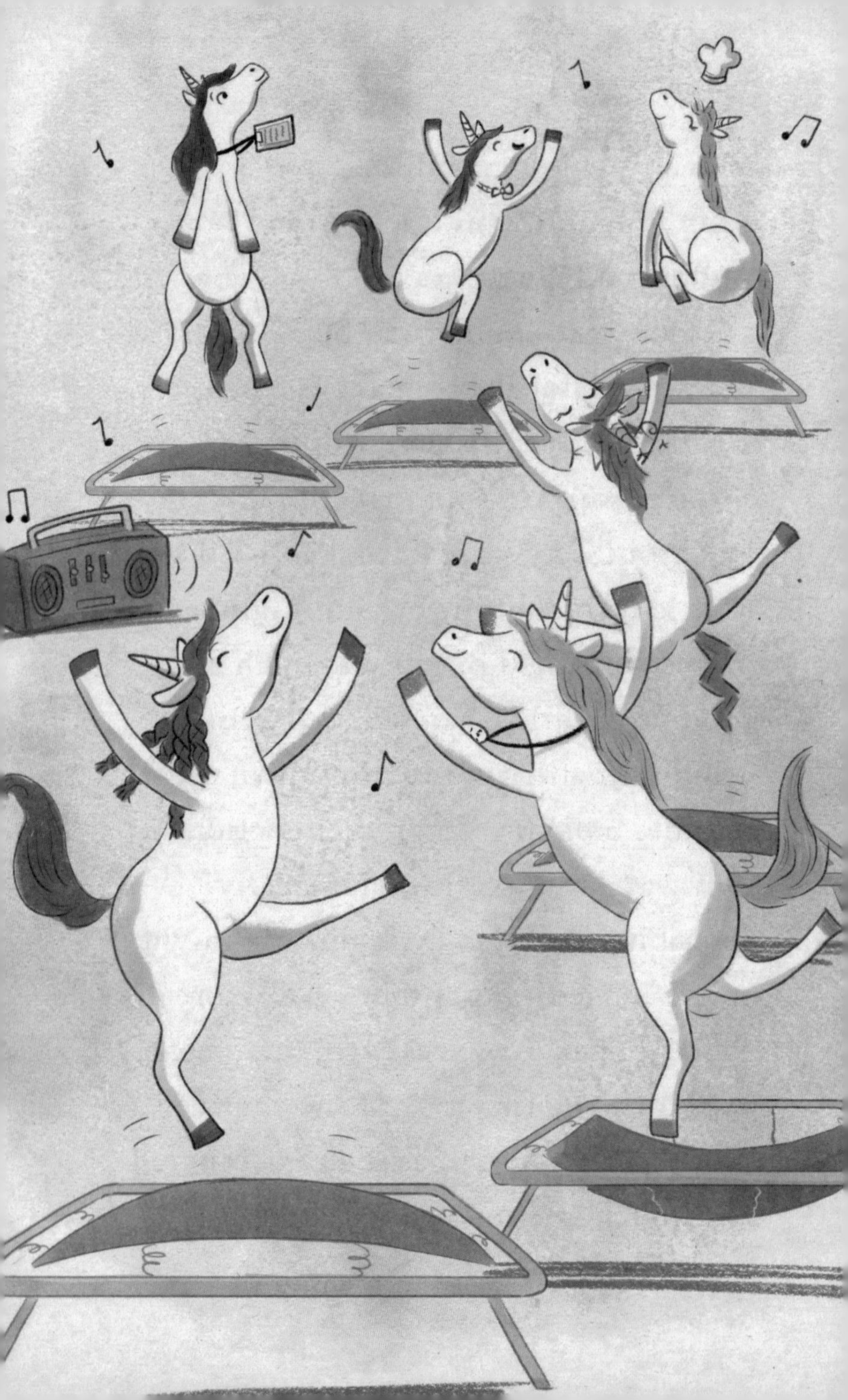

nothing like the feeling of bouncing around on a trampoline surrounded by your own unicorn magic!

Rose began following Lightning's instructions for the next section of the routine, leaping into the air on one hoof, spinning in a figure of eight, then landing on the other hoof. Except that when she landed, her leg slipped and bent backwards, sending pain shooting through her body.

"Oww!" she said softly, lying on the trampoline for a moment and trying not to make a fuss.

The other unicorns soon realized what had happened and galloped over.

"Don't move," said Indigo, shifting into their role as Safety Officer. Indigo jumped off their trampoline and went over to kneel down beside Rose.

"I'm fine. I was just testing out a different kind of move – it's called the Collapsing Unicorn!" Rose joked. But when she tried to move, she found she couldn't. She hated to admit it, but it felt as if her leg might be broken! Indigo inspected her leg, gently turning it to see how bad the damage was.

"We'll get a stretcher and carry you back to the stables," Indigo said, as she placed Rose's leg down. "You'll have to rest for a few days at least."

"But what about all the food for sports day?" said Rose. "I need every second I've got to prepare it all…"

Indigo shook their head. "It's more important that you rest than make the food," they said. "Otherwise it might take even longer to recover."

Indigo looked so serious that Rose gulped. She'd been really looking forward

to creating a sports day feast too. What were the guests going to eat if she couldn't cook for them?

"I know it's frustrating," said Scarlett. "But the rest of us can take care of Truly Tasty while you're out of action."

Rose gulped harder now. She'd eaten the other unicorns' food before, and, if she was honest, she'd prefer to eat her own tail. But it seemed that she had no other choice!

Chapter 6

On Top of the Rainbow

Ming snuggled into her duvet as she woke up, enjoying the soft, flower-scented covers. The bed in her lodge was so cosy, and she wished she could stay here rather than go outside and practise more sports. There were two days to go until the sports day and things hadn't got any better. She was certain the centaurs thought she was terrible at all the sports they'd been practising, although they hadn't said it to her face, of course. She made herself feel better by remembering that in *three* days there would be a full moon, and she'd be able to go home.

Her stomach fluttered with panic. But what if she couldn't? Ming thought the reason she couldn't jump back before was because the moon was only partially visible, but she didn't know that for certain. What if she had to wait longer – or if she couldn't go home at all?

Ming felt tears prickle at her eyes. She shook her head and hopped out from under the covers. She wasn't going to be upset about it and she didn't want

to feel sorry for herself. Especially when she was pretty sure that the unicorns had created the sports day to keep her busy for the week until she could go home. It seemed they had no idea Ming wasn't really a sporty kind of creature.

She took a shower and headed to Truly Tasty, where she'd arranged to meet the rest of her team that morning. The four centaurs were already sitting at a table when she arrived, looking a little grumpy.

"Is everything OK?" Ming asked, hopping towards them.

"We're still waiting for our breakfast." Cecil grimaced. Then he waved a hand as Scarlett came out of the kitchen carrying four plates. "Oh, look, I think that's it!"

Scarlett trotted over. "I'm sorry for the delay. Chef Rose has injured her leg so the rest of us unicorns are looking after the kitchen."

"Oh no! Is she OK?" Ming asked.

Scarlett gave a little smile. "I think so, but she has to rest it for now. Hopefully she'll be back to Truly Tasty really soon!"

The red-haired unicorn bustled away with a swish of her tail and the centaurs began munching on their hay-hash browns breakfast.

"We were talking about what sports to practise today, Ming," said Cedric. "We haven't tried the Rainbow Relay yet, so we think we should start with that."

Ming tried to smile. "OK," she said as brightly as she could manage. "Will it be in the sports arena?"

Sirnam shook her head and pointed upwards. "Nope – it's on the rainbow!"

Ming followed her finger to look upwards.

High in the
sky of Sparkle
Valley, a
beautiful
rainbow
arched
between the
fluffy clouds, the arches
finishing at different ends of the valley.
"Up there?" she squeaked.

"Uh-huh," Serendipity replied. "Each of us has to run back and forth across it once, then pass the baton to the next team member to do the same, until we've all crossed it."

"We're fast runners," said Cedric, "so we really should win this one!"

Sirnam nodded. "But we need to win *everything*," she said, "if we want to ensure we're awarded the overall sports day trophy!"

"Oh, yes," Serendipity added. "I heard

the trophy is a gold unicorn statue! It would look stunning at the entrance to our stables back at home. We *have* to win."

Ming decided to have something from the breakfast buffet, rather than give the unicorns more cooking to do, and nibbled at a bowl of carrot-cake cereal. Then the team trotted – or in Ming's case, hopped – towards the southern end of the rainbow, past the Shimmer Sports Park and Shoot for the Stars, the theme park that floated above Sparkle Valley.

Ming wondered if there'd be a pot of gold at the end of the rainbow, because she'd heard legends about finding such things. She grinned when she saw she was right, sort of: there *was* a golden pot by the base of the rainbow, and it was filled with golden batons. The unicorns must have put it there so that creatures could practise the relay.

Cecil reached in and took out a baton, and Ming went to do the same. "No, we can only have one baton between us, Ming," Cecil told her. "That's the point of the relay – we have to pass the baton between us!"

Ming shrunk back, feeling embarrassed. She wasn't to know – she hadn't ever run in a race before, let alone a relay one! "Sorry," she said quietly.

"The fastest of us should go first and last," Serendipity said. "That's important in a relay race. Ming, are you happy to go third, in the middle?"

Ming nodded, although "happy" was probably an exaggeration. But all she had to do was run over the rainbow and back, she told herself. That couldn't be so hard, could it?

She watched as Cecil began galloping

over the rainbow first, the baton clasped tightly in his hand. It took him just seconds to reach the other side, his long white tail flailing out behind him. He spun on his back hooves and galloped back towards the rest of the team, where Sirnam was waiting to take the baton. She reached out, grabbed it from Cecil, then raced across the rainbow herself.

Ming hopped into position, ready for when Sirnam came back, so she could take the baton from her. Ming's heart beat faster as Sirnam cantered over the rainbow towards her. *Don't drop the baton!* she told herself.

Sirnam slowed as she reached Ming and she took the baton in both front paws. But it was too big to hold, so she tucked it under her arm instead, squeezing it tightly. She began scampering over the rainbow, which was rubbery and easy to run on. She realized it felt a bit like the moon!

Ming smiled as she neared the other end. She slowed down so she could turn round before reaching it. She didn't want to fall off! She spun like the centaurs as best as she could, and began racing back across towards them. But she heard them yell in horror and look down. What was wrong?

And then she realized. She'd dropped the baton! It must have slipped from under

her arm when she'd spun back. She stopped running and looked down, seeing it way below her on the ground, shining as it lay on the grass. Her heart sank to her silver bushy tail.

As Ming looked at the centaurs, who were all shaking their heads, she spotted the pale moon rising in the distance behind them. She gazed at it, wishing more than anything she was back there.

Just three more days and I'll be home! she told herself.

CHAPTER 7

Ming to the Rescue

"It can't be that hard," Lightning said to Amber in the kitchen of Truly Tasty the next day. "All we have to do is follow Rose's recipes!"

Amber frowned as she peered at the list Rose had written out for them. "But I don't know what half of these ingredients are. Do *you* know what a sky blossom is? Or a candy clove?"

Lightning came over and looked at the

list in Amber's hoof. "Don't worry – we'll work it out!"

The unicorns had been taking it in turns to cook the meals in Truly Tasty ever since Rose had hurt her leg. Luckily, they were all recipes the unicorns knew well, because Rose had served them at Sparkle Valley for years. It took them longer, but they were just about keeping on top of the orders in the kitchen.

The recipes for the sports-day food were a different matter, though – they were *all* new. Amber wished she were back at the Sunshine Spa, where she loved pampering creatures with treatments, from scale scrubs to wing wraps, hoof baths to beak cleansers. She'd kept to her promise of giving Ming lots of treatments too – in fact, this morning the moon rabbit had visited to have a foot and tail massage. But

Ming had been really quiet and Amber guessed she was still missing home, despite their attempts to distract her.

Lightning was lining up jars of ingredients on the bench in front of them, ready to make the first recipe: speedy-strength starlight scones.

Just as he was about to pour the first jar into the bowl on the scales, Scarlett came rushing in.

"Oh good, you're both here," said Scarlett. "I need your help! Quickly!"

Amber spun round on her back hooves, surprised. Scarlett was usually the calmest of the unicorns. If she was panicking about something, it couldn't be good.

"The team of obakes are arguing with the selkies about the sports day," Scarlett explained. "The obakes think they should be allowed to shapeshift into anything they want to help them compete, but the selkies think that's cheating. We didn't decide on the rules for that, did we?"

Lightning dropped the jar he'd been holding. "Argh – we should have thought of this!" He shook his head in annoyance, making his yellow mane swoosh about. "I'll come with you and speak to them."

"But what about the recipes?" Amber said.

Lightning was already at the door with

Scarlett. "I'll be back as soon as I can," he told her. "Everything is ready for the starlight scones, so you can make those while I'm gone."

"Wait—" Amber started to say, but Lightning and Scarlett had disappeared.

Amber frowned at the ingredients set out in front of her. She didn't recognize any of them. But, as Lightning had said, he'd already prepared everything, so how hard could it be?

"It's *lovely*," said Indigo later that day. They'd popped into the Truly Tasty kitchen for a snack, and Amber had asked them to try the speedy-strength starlight scones.

But the expression on Indigo's face did *not* match their words.

"Really?" asked Amber, putting her

front hooves to her mouth. "They taste really, really salty to me…"

"Well, maybe a bit." Indigo chewed on the scone, their face screwing up.

"I knew it!" said Amber. Lightning had left out the jar of mermaid tears for the recipe, but she hadn't been sure about using them because they were *incredibly* salty. She grabbed the tray of scones and tipped them all into the compost bin. "There's no way we can serve these to the guests."

A knock at the kitchen door made the two unicorns spin round.

"Come in," said Amber, hoping harder than ever it was Rose.

But of course Rose wouldn't have knocked at her own kitchen. It was Ming.

"Hi, Ming," Amber said, trying not to sound stressed. "Are you hungry? Truly

Tasty isn't open at the moment, but I can find you a snack…"

Ming shook her head. "No, I'm not hungry – don't worry! I was wondering if you needed any help. You were chatting about making everything here this morning during my lovely massage and sounded quite worried about it all."

"You can cook?" Amber said, her heart lifting.

Ming waggled her ears and smiled. "I can – with the help of my moon magic! There isn't much that's edible on the moon, you see, but my magic helps me to make anything tasty."

"Even this?" asked Indigo. They held out the salty scone.

"I can try!" said Ming. "What flavour would you like?"

Indigo licked their lips.

"Banana-toffee-walnut-cocoa, please!"

Ming nodded slowly, then fluttered her ears, making sparks fizz around them. She sent the sparks towards the scone in Indigo's hoof.

"Try it now," Ming said.

Indigo paused. They really didn't want another super-salty mouthful. But as they brought it to their mouth they could smell that it was different. Indigo took a little bite and delicious flavours flooded into their mouth – exactly as they'd asked for. "That's amazing!"

Amber was jumping from hoof to hoof in excitement. "Ming, you're incredible! Please, please, *please* say you'll stay and help with the other recipes!"

Ming beamed. "I'll try my best," she said.

She'd left the centaurs practising for the River Radiant Swim, galloping like greyhounds through the water, and was happy not to rush back there. If she could help out the unicorns instead, that seemed more important. She pushed away the worry that the centaurs would be annoyed at her.

They probably haven't even noticed I'm not there, she decided.

CHAPTER 8

Hiding Away

That evening, Ming couldn't fall asleep, no matter what she did. She tried counting starlight sheep and using the camomile-calm sleep mask on her bedside table, but she still found herself wide awake at two o'clock in the morning. She was too worried about the sports day, which would begin in nine hours' time, and letting the centaurs down. She'd felt fine earlier in the afternoon when she'd been helping the unicorns in the kitchen — she'd barely thought about it. But now thoughts of sports disasters whirled in her head.

Giving up on sleep, Ming hopped out of bed and opened the curtains of her lodge. Right outside her window, the moon was shining brightly. It was so nearly full too! She stared up at it, wondering what to do.

She just wanted to hide away until she could get home…

An idea pinged into Ming's head. Maybe that was it! Ming could tell a little fib and say she wasn't feeling well — which wasn't exactly a lie anyway, because she felt

a bit sick at the thought of competing in the sports day. She hopped into the living area and the little candles on the walls lit up magically. Ming went to the desk in the corner, where a pad of goose-glitter paper and the firebird-feather pen were lying. She shuffled on to the chair and began to write:

To the centaurs,
I'm afraid I'm not feeling very well and won't be able to join in the sports day. Please say I'm sorry I'm missing it to the unicorns. Good luck – I'm sure you'll win!

Ming

She picked up an envelope, folded the note and slipped it inside. Before she could change her mind, she scampered out of her lodge towards the centaurs', which was at the end of the same row. It was pitch-dark outside – thick clouds must have drifted over the moon now, but Ming was used to seeing in the dark. She hopped up the steps silently and leaned the note against the door.

Quickly, she spun round and padded down the steps, careful not to make a sound.

◐

The unicorns met in Shimmer Sports Park at nine o' clock – everyone apart from Rose, who still needed to rest her broken leg. There were still some last-minute jobs to take care of – organizing the team bibs, which were different colours, and setting up drinks tables at every sports location to make sure all the sports-creatures could keep hydrated.

Lightning felt a drop of rain and looked up at the sky. The clouds seemed to be looming and showed no signs of shifting.

"It can't rain, not today!" he cried. "Scarlett, can you do something with your magic?"

The unicorn shook her head, her red mane swooshing from side to side. "You know magic can't control the weather," she said calmly. "Anyway, if it was sunny, everyone would get really hot. It's better for it to be a bit cloudy."

"I guess," Lightning said. He just wanted everything to go perfectly. Out of the corner of his eye, he saw a centaur trotting into the arena. "You're a little early," he called out, suprised to see Serendipity.

"The opening ceremony doesn't start until eleven!"

Serendipity galloped over. "I wanted to let you know that Ming is unwell," she said. "She said she's sorry she'll be missing the sports day." The half-horse, half-human creature held out the note she'd found outside their lodge that morning.

Lightning took it and read the message. "Poor Ming," he said, then looked up at Serendipity. "I'm afraid it's too late to reorganize the teams, so your team will be one creature down."

Serendipity shrugged. "That's OK." Deep down, she thought they probably had a better chance without Ming anyway. But then she felt bad for having those thoughts. Had Ming realized that? It had been pretty obvious the centaurs were much better at every sport than her.

"You go and have a good breakfast before the sports day starts," Lightning said. "Thanks for letting us know about Ming."

As Serendipity galloped away, Indigo came over, pulling a cart full of water jugs behind them.

"Is everything OK?" they asked Lightning.

"Ming's not feeling well," he replied. "But the centaurs will be OK without her, I think."

Indigo frowned. "What's wrong with Ming?"

Lightning showed Indigo the note. "She didn't say." He nodded to the water jugs.

"Are there many of those left to put out?"

Indigo didn't answer. They were still looking at the note. "I think I should go and check on her," they said, unclipping the cart from their back and cantering towards the arena's exit.

"But what about the water jugs?" Lightning shouted behind Indigo.

"Can you put them out?" they called back without looking round, then, without waiting for an answer, added, "Thank you!"

Indigo raced towards the lodges. They wanted to make sure Ming was OK, and it wouldn't take long. After all, no one knew exactly how sick she was. As Safety Officer, Indigo wanted to check that Ming was safe and didn't need anything.

When Indigo arrived at the lodge area, they realized they didn't know which lodge was Ming's. Indigo spun round on their hooves, trying to remember. Then they spotted a centaur walking past.

"Hey!" Indigo said to Cedric, waving a hoof. "Do you know which is Ming's lodge?"

The centaur trotted over and pointed to the lodge at the end of the row. It was a small one, because Ming wasn't a big creature and there was only one of her. It was impressive how Scarlett used magic to resize each lodge to ensure it fitted each group of guests.

Indigo galloped to the lodge and knocked on the door. They waited, shuffling from hoof to hoof, but there was no answer. They put an ear to the door and couldn't hear anything inside.

"Ming? Are you there?" Indigo called, starting to panic a little bit.

"Shall I ram the door down?" Cedric suggested, cantering up behind them.

"No! Let's save that as a last resort," Indigo replied quickly. They were sure Scarlett's magic would be able to fix a broken door, but they were worried they'd scare Ming if she was inside.

"Ming!" Indigo called again. "Please just let us know you're OK!"

Chapter 9

Sports Day Solution

Ming lay in bed, listening to Indigo calling to her from outside. It didn't sound as if the unicorn was going to go away if Ming didn't answer. Then she heard Cedric suggest he could break down the door!

She sat up at that, then swung her feet to the floor and took a deep breath into her belly. Ming thought about pretending to be sick, but could she really lie to their faces? She already felt really bad about fibbing in the note to the centaurs.

She hopped slowly to the door, took another long breath and opened it a crack.

"Ming!" Indigo said with a face full of concern. "Are you OK? I heard you were sick…"

Ming lowered her head, knowing she couldn't lie. "Well, it's just… I mean … I'm not sick… I didn't know what to do…"

"What do you mean?" Indigo asked.

"I don't know how to explain it," Ming said quietly. Her heart thrummed with panic. How would she tell Indigo how she was really feeling?

"Look, if you'd prefer we left you alone, then we absolutely can." Indigo spoke so gently that Ming felt tears come to her eyes. "I only wanted to check you were OK."

Ming couldn't help it – she burst into tears.

"Oh, Ming, what's wrong?" Indigo

asked as the little moon rabbit opened the door wider.

Ming let Indigo hug her, and sobbed in their embrace.

"It's just … I want to go home," Ming managed to say. "And I'm terrible at sports. I tried – I really did, especially when I realized you'd probably put on the sports day specially for me. But I've never done any sports before. I knew I was going to let the centaurs down. It's OK playing for fun, but not when everyone wants to win so badly."

Cedric had been quiet up until now, but Ming heard his deep voice say, "I'm so sorry we made you feel that way, Ming!"

The moon rabbit looked up at the towering centaur. "It's OK," she said. "You didn't know. I don't blame you for wanting to win. It's just not really my thing."

Indigo stared at the ground, deep in thought. "I'm very sorry too," they said. "I think we need to make some changes. We should have realized that not all creatures would enjoy competing in a sports day. Ming, if I promise you won't have to join in unless you really want to, will you come with us? I think it'd be helpful if the other unicorns hear how you've been feeling."

Ming nodded, her tall bunny ears flapping. She suddenly felt as light as a cloud now that she'd admitted what had been wrong, and Indigo had been so understanding. She didn't feel like hiding away any more.

"So we'll have a sports day without any prizes?" Lightning said, screwing up his face in confusion.

Ming had explained to the unicorns

how she'd been feeling, and Indigo had put forward their idea to alter the sports day.

Indigo shook their head, their mane flicking from side to side. "We can still have competitive sports and award the trophy. But we can also have some that the creatures can play for fun, and no one has to play at all if they'd prefer not to. They can watch instead, or enjoy other parts of Sparkle Valley."

"That sounds like the perfect solution," said Scarlett. "I can use magic to change some of the sports so they're not all about winning. And we can do some special things for the spectators, like make flags for them to wave and create a sports-day song for them to sing."

"Oh, that sounds like so much fun," Amber said, spinning on the spot. "I can do the flags! I have some pretty pink material that would be perfect…"

Basil raised a hoof. "And I'll come up with the song!"

Lightning looked at the watch on his hoof. It was ten thirty a.m. "You'll make up a song in thirty minutes?" he asked.

Basil grinned. "I bet I can do it in twenty!" he replied. "Thinking about it, we've been so serious about this whole sports-day thing, trying to make it the best. Somehow, along the way, we've all forgotten it's supposed to be fun!"

Ming listened to the unicorns discuss their plan with a smile on her face. This sounded like a sports day for everyone. She even felt a bit excited at the thought of watching the other creatures play sports. But not as excited as she felt about going home. The worry about getting back popped into her head again, but she tried to ignore it. She had a sports day to enjoy between now and then, after all.

Chapter 10

A Tasty End

Half an hour later, all the creatures in Sparkle Valley had crowded into the Shimmer Sports Park arena. Ming sat happily near the back, next to the centaurs. They insisted on sitting with her, even though she was no longer part of their team.

"I'm so sorry," Serendipity said to Ming for the twentieth time. "I hate that we made you feel bad."

"Please don't worry," Ming replied. "You didn't know – and it's all worked out in the end!"

Music suddenly blared and the unicorns appeared, each trotting to one of the trampolines at the centre of the arena.

Scarlett held a microphone and began to speak as the music faded again. "Welcome to the first-ever Sparkle Valley Sports Day," she declared. "It's going to be a little different from what we had originally planned. We want all creatures to know that they don't have to participate if they don't want to, and we have a lot of fun things planned for our spectators! And if you'd like to play sports but would prefer not to compete against others, we have some special activities planned for those creatures too. That's what's going to make this the best sports day ever – you can be

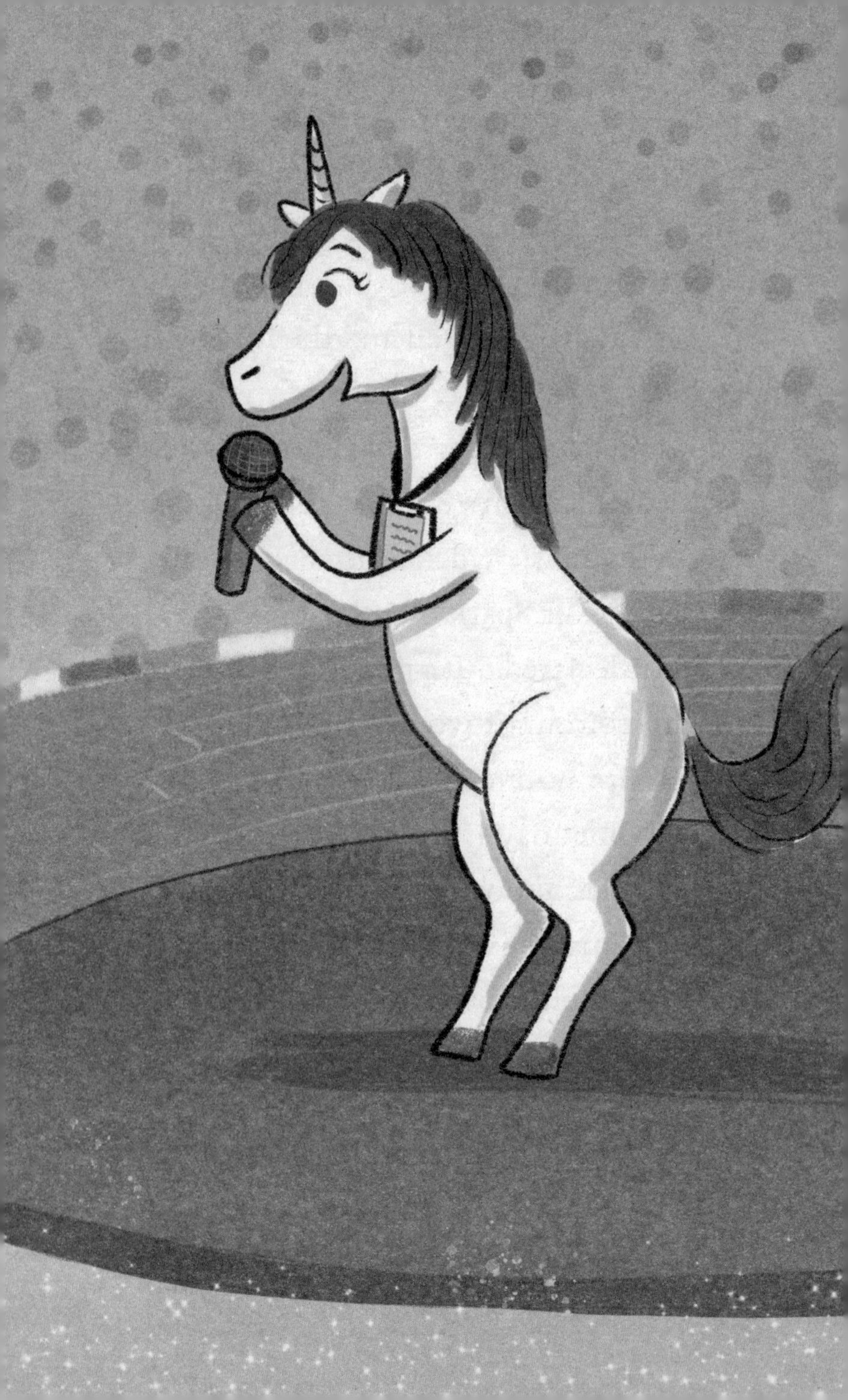

involved as much or as little as you want!"

The audience burst into applause. A group of fauns sitting in front of Ming hugged each other. "What a relief!" one of them said.

Lightning took the microphone. "To start the day, we have an opening performance for you. Our very own synchronized sparkle trampolining!"

The music started again and the unicorns all began to bounce in time with each other. Everyone except Chef Rose, of course. Ming hoped she was doing OK.

The unicorns' performance was extremely impressive, with lots of spins and jumps, completely synchronized. As Ming watched on, she wondered if she might try it one day – with all the jumping, this looked like the kind of sport she might actually enjoy! As the unicorns moved, their magic sparkled from their horns and fluttered outwards, so that it reached every part of the arena. They finished with a quadruple spin and a star jump, and the crowd roared with appreciation.

Afterwards, the teams competing in the sports day went to get ready for the first event. The creatures who wanted to play sports but only for fun went off to the sport of their choosing, which left the creatures

who wanted to watch the sports day. Ming was relieved to see at least twenty creatures left in the arena – she wasn't the only one who preferred to watch rather than play!

Scarlett used her magic to resize the arena to fit them better, and Amber gave out the flags she'd made, covered in pink and purple stars. Basil taught them his special sports-day song, "Jump, Spin, Dash and Dive in Sparkle Valley", and they enjoyed the snacks that Ming had helped to make in the kitchen yesterday – including her favourite, raindrop-rose long-and-shortbread.

Ming had a magical day watching all the teams compete, hopping from the River Radiant Swim to the Rainbow Relay to Fizz-Foot Hockey. She cheered for everyone, but hardest for the centaurs, especially when they were declared the winners at the end of the day!

As the centaurs were presented with the life-size gold unicorn statue and everyone in the arena clapped loudly, a pink-haired unicorn appeared on the stage: Chef Rose! She was hobbling a bit but smiling. Behind her, Indigo and Amber pulled a cart piled high with something covered by a bright purple cloth.

Rose took the microphone. "I'm sorry I haven't been around to make your meals this week. I'd planned all sorts of sports-day treats, but I had to rest as I hurt my leg. The other unicorns have tried their best, but it took someone special to save the day." Rose searched the arena, and her eyes landed on Ming. "Ming, please will you come to the stage?"

The moon rabbit felt her whole body heat up with embarrassment as all the creatures looked at her. But Rose was smiling so gratefully at her that Ming wanted to go and join her on the stage. It felt a lot different from a few days ago, when she'd been called up to the stage to meet the rest of her team.

Ming hopped down towards Chef Rose, who gave her the biggest hug when she arrived.

"Thank you so very, very much!" Rose said into Ming's ear.

The chef turned to Indigo and Amber, nodding. They whipped the cover off the cart to reveal a huge pink-and-purple cake – in the

shape of a unicorn head. It was even bigger than the unicorn statue, and looked extremely tasty.

"This is a very special cake," Rose went on. "It has magic in it, which means that whatever your favourite cake flavour is, it'll taste of that when you eat it! The other unicorns told me that without Ming it would have never been made. And there's enough for everyone – come up and get a slice!"

Rose began cutting the cake. "You have to try it first, Ming!" She slid a piece of the cake on to a lily-pad plate and passed it to Ming. The moon rabbit looked at it with uncertainty. Even though she'd helped to make it, she wasn't convinced it really would taste of her favourite: lunar-lemon sponge with starshine-cream icing.

She lifted her fork to her mouth… It did!

It *really* did! Wow, this was a very special way to end her last day at Sparkle Valley. That's if she could get home tomorrow…

◐

Ming was the first creature to get to the gates of Sparkle Valley the next morning, with her moon-shaped backpack hooked around her shoulders. She'd barely slept a wink. She wasn't sure if it was because she'd been worrying about being able to jump back to the moon, or because she'd eaten so much unicorn cake she had a bit of a tummy ache.

Two griffins, still standing guard at the gate, nodded to her in an official way. Ming looked back at Sparkle Valley and saw the unicorns all galloping towards her.

"We wanted to say goodbye!" Basil called out.

As Ming smiled at them, she realized something. She'd enjoyed a lot of her time

in Sparkle Valley and maybe she would come back one day. It had been good for her to see other creatures and make some new friends – even if she did like her life by herself on the moon.

As if Indigo had read Ming's thoughts, they held up something in their hoof. Ming hopped closer and saw it was an eyelash! Creatures could only visit

Sparkle Valley if they were sent a unicorn eyelash, so this was very special indeed.

"We'd love for you to come back one day," Indigo said. "And we promise we won't make you play any sports!"

Ming grinned. "Thank you. I promise I will come and visit again. I'd like to try synchronized sparkle trampolining – and eat some more of Chef Rose's amazing cakes!"

Rose nodded. "I'll make as many cakes as you can eat! Although I really wouldn't recommend doing both at the same time," she joked.

Ming gratefully took the unicorn eyelash from Indigo. She placed it in her backpack, then checked the skies above.

It was the moment of truth. The moon was fully visible now – a faint but clear full circle above the top of the mountain at the north of Sparkle Valley. Ming realized she was trembling from her ears to her tail. Would it work this time?

There was nothing left to do but try. Ming tried to smile at the unicorns as she bent her knees and crouched down low, then she took the deepest breath, trying to ignore the worries swirling in her mind.

She pushed off from her rear feet, looking up at the moon as she leaped…

Yes!

Ming found herself zooming upwards, heading towards the moon in a giant jump.

"Thank you!" she called down to the unicorns, who were beaming at her and waving furiously.

Ming gave them one last wave and turned back to the moon, growing bigger

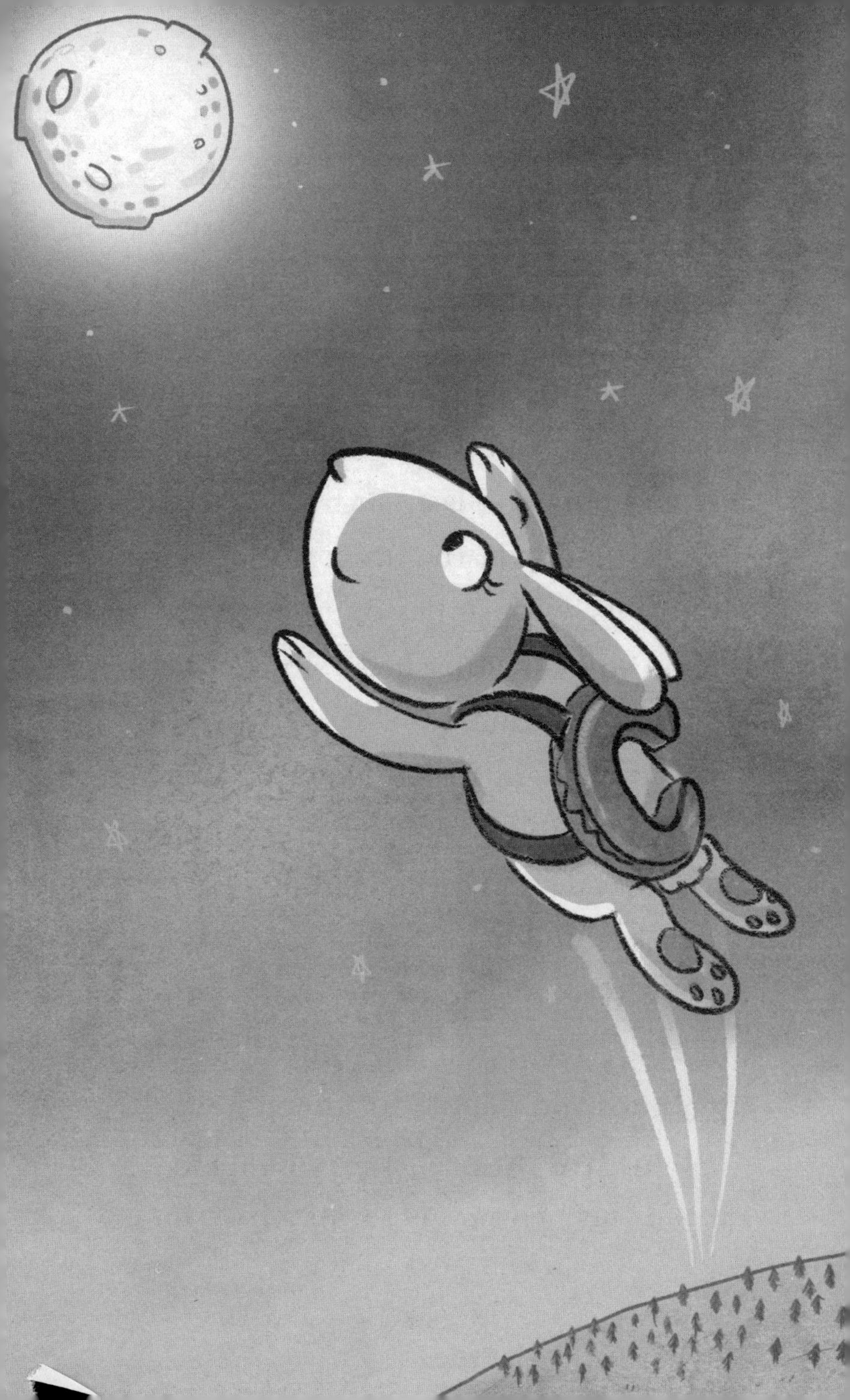

and bigger as she got closer. Seconds later, it was so large she couldn't see anything else, and she put out her feet to make sure she landed safely. She touched down, feeling the springy moon ground beneath her, and rolled over to hug it. She was home, at last.

Back on Earth, the unicorns looked at each other with smiles on their faces.

"I'm so glad Ming had a good time in the end," said Indigo.

"And made us realize how silly we were to try to make everyone compete in the sports day!" Basil added.

Scarlett nodded in agreement. "We'll certainly keep a closer eye on how our guests are feeling in the future." She held up a hoof and the others joined her.

"Unicorns, unite!" they said as they tapped their feet together in a high-hoof.

It had been a very busy week, but they'd learned a lot. Running a holiday park wasn't always easy, but the unicorns couldn't imagine doing anything else!

Discover more from The Unicorns of Sparkle Valley in *Frozen Spell*

Keep reading for a sneak peek...

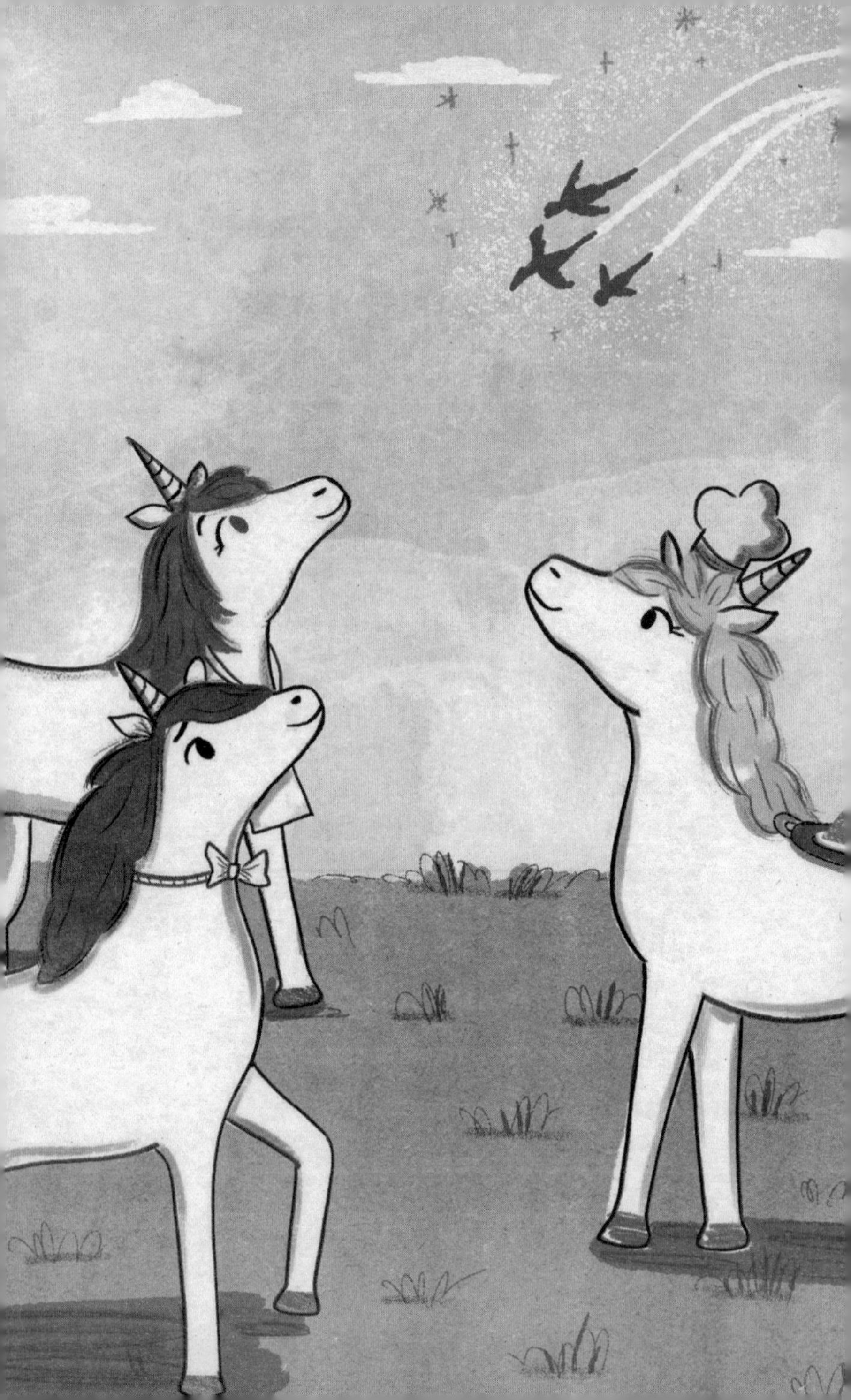

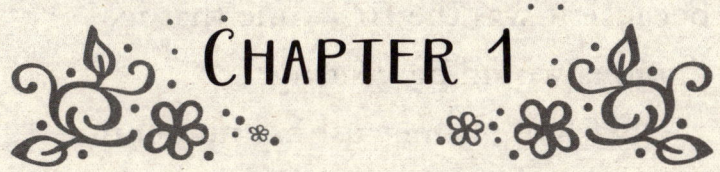

Chapter 1

New Arrivals

"I can see them!" Basil yelled as he stared up at the perfect blue sky.

Scarlett tipped back her head, her orange-red mane sparkling in the sunlight. She could only see three little silvery dots in the sky at first. But as they came closer, she could make out flapping wings and long, spiky tails.

The unicorns were always happy when new guests arrived at Sparkle Valley, the magical holiday park they ran together. But today they were particularly excited, because it was the first time that ice dragons would be visiting.

Chef Rose came rushing up behind them while expertly balancing a tray on her back.

"Nice timing," she said. "Or should I say 'ice timing', ha! These polar-peak pastries are fresh out of the oven."

"Great work, Rose," said Scarlett with a nod. She ticked off "welcome snacks" on her clipboard.

The ice dragons swooped lower, their wings guiding them to land gently at the grand gated entrance of the holiday park.

"Wow!" the smallest one squealed. "Sparkle Valley is huge – and *everything* is sparkly!"

With wide beams on their faces,

Rose, Scarlett and Basil trotted towards the shimmering silver gate, which rose magically to let the dragons through.

"Welcome to Sparkle Valley," Scarlett said with a big smile. "The most magical place in the universe."

All three ice dragons smiled back.

"We're really here!" said the smallest dragon. He was dark green, and his bright green eyes glowed with awe and excitement. "Oh, and I have the eyelash!" He held up something tiny in his claw.

A larger dragon with glimmering pale-blue eyes said to him, "Thank you, Iggy." Then she turned to Scarlett and her friends. "We couldn't believe it when he opened the envelope that arrived on our cave porch and found the unicorn lash. He's been talking about it non-stop ever since — we all have. It's the first time we've been on holiday. Usually, we're at home caring for our parents, who aren't very well and struggle to fly. Thank you for inviting us, and for arranging their care while we are here!"

All sorts of magical creatures came to stay at Sparkle Valley — but only if they received a unicorn eyelash in the post. No amount of coins, gold, diamonds or rubies would buy a trip, although plenty of creatures who'd wanted to come had tried! The eyelash invite system meant that the unicorns could invite the guests who most deserved a holiday to Sparkle Valley. By using Scarlett's magic ball, the unicorns could find out who was most in need around the world.

Rose trotted forward. "Please enjoy a polar-peak pastry. I made them especially for your arrival!"

"Rose is our incredible chef," Scarlett explained as the ice dragons carefully used their claws to take a sugar-dusted, pyramid-shaped pastry from the tray. "She'll be making sure you eat like royalty while you're here! Basil is Entertainment Officer, and he has a lot of fun activities planned for you. I'm Scarlett, and I'm in charge of the magic in Sparkle Valley."

Basil twirled on the spot. "You're going to have the best holiday of your lives," he said brightly, "starting with a talent show tonight!"

"Ooh," said all three ice dragons in unison.

"Speaking of which ... I need to go and put the final touches to the preparations for the show." Basil clicked his hind hooves together and cantered away as he called back, "See youuuuuuu later!"

"I'd better go too," Rose said. "Unicorn magic makes cooking a lot easier, but I still need to keep an eye on things in the kitchen! I'll see you all at dinner."

The ice dragons waved goodbye to Basil and Rose.

Scarlett held out her clipboard again. "Before the fun starts, I need to check you in. We have to keep track of who's here at the park for safety reasons, you see. Can you give me your names, please?"

"I'm Iggy," said the smallest dragon. "That's my older sister, Iris, and my even older brother, Isaac. I'm super excited – I've never been on holiday before!" He flapped his wings so hard that he hovered above the ground.

Scarlett grinned at the delightful little ice dragon. "Perfect," she said. "Then let's get your tour of Sparkle Valley started!"

She led the way along the long, winding drive, which was lined with sparkling palm trees. The ice dragons followed and, every so often, Iggy yelped with joy as he spotted something exciting.

They arrived at the ice dragons' lodge first. It was extremely big – which was important, as the ice dragons needed space to stretch out their wings while they slept. The glittering wooden lodge was draped in green vines with pretty red flowers that hung down the outside walls.

"It's so pretty!" said Iris, nodding. "And big! We didn't know if you'd have anywhere that would fit us."

"You didn't need to worry about that," Scarlett replied gently. "I make sure our accommodation always fits our guests, with a spell or two!"

Iggy eagerly skipped into the lodge. "I'm going to choose my bedroom!" he squealed, his green tail jiggling.

"This bed is so bouncy!" the others heard Iggy call from inside.

"Be careful!" Iris shouted after her younger brother. "Please don't break anything!"

She shook her head, but there was a smile on her face. She and Isaac followed their brother inside, to drop off their luggage and have a quick look around.

"This bed is so bouncy!" Iggy yelled again with glee.

Scarlett grinned. She loved to see guests so excited. It reminded her to never forget just how special Sparkle Valley was.

"The lodge is wonderful," said Isaac as he and Iris walked back out. "So sleek and spacious!"

Iggy was still bouncing on the bed inside, so Scarlett called loudly enough for him to hear, "Next stop, Rainbow Water Park!"

Sure enough, Iggy came rushing out, skidding to a halt beside them.

"Wait for me!" he said.

Scarlett trotted towards the north side of Sparkle Valley, where a large snow-topped mountain towered towards the sky. A sparkling rainbow shone out from its peak, arching high above them, all the way to a mountain on the opposite side of the valley.

As they got closer, the ice dragons could see the water park properly. It was set into the side of the snowy mountain and had too many pools to count – huge ones with diving boards, smaller ones that whirled with bubbles, pools under waterfalls and narrow pools that hugged the mountainside.

"We use magic to make sure we have a pool for every temperature preference. From super hot to extra icy!" Scarlett explained.

"I can't wait to soak my tired wings after our long journey," sighed Iris.

Next, Scarlett took them to Shimmer Sports Park, which offered every kind of sport imaginable, and some that the ice dragons had never heard of, including Fizz-Foot Hockey and Twirl Tennis.

Iggy wanted to try the Galloping Go-Karts immediately, until Scarlett mentioned Shoot for the Stars – Sparkle Valley's theme park that was magically suspended in the sky.

Scarlett suggested she drop them off

at the theme park so they could enjoy it properly, as she had some work to do.

"I'll leave you here," she said as they arrived at the entrance to Shoot for the Stars: an arched doorway made of sparkling clouds. "But this evening we'd love you to join us for the talent show at the Sky Stage, on the south-west side of the valley. Lots of our guests will be performing!"

Isaac's lilac eyes gleamed. "We'll be there! Is it too late to sign up?"

"Not at all," Scarlett replied, passing them a map of Sparkle Valley. "Just be there by seven o'clock, and we'll make sure you're on the list to perform. I'll see you then!"

She waved goodbye to the ice dragons and galloped off to help with the talent-show preparations.

If you liked *The Unicorns of Sparkle Valley*, explore more from Catherine Coe in The Unicorns of Blossom Wood series: